T0198980

The Tale of
Loveth
and
Diana

Ng Dagreat

AuthorHouse™ UK
1663 Liberty Drive
Bloomington, IN 47403 USA
www.authorhouse.co.uk
UK TFN: 0800 0148641 (Toll Free inside the UK)
UK Local: 02036 956322 (+44 20 3695 6322 from outside the UK)

Because of the dynamic nature of the Internet, any web addresses or links contained in this book may have changed
since publication and may no longer be valid. The views expressed in this work are solely those of the author and do
not necessarily reflect the views of the publisher, and the publisher hereby disclaims any responsibility for them.

Any people depicted in stock imagery provided by Getty Images are models,
and such images are being used for illustrative purposes only.
Certain stock imagery © Getty Images.

This book is printed on acid-free paper.

ISBN: 978-1-6655-8844-7 (sc)
ISBN: 978-1-6655-8845-4 (e)

Print information available on the last page.

Published by AuthorHouse 04/16/2021

authorHOUSE®

The Tale of
Loveth
and
Diana

Alex had two siblings, named Loveth and Diana. They lived in a town called Eden situated in a country. Alex lived in a city named Dallas with his two sisters, Daddy and Mummy.

Their house was close to a castle.
They loved the court where the
young prince and family lived.

The girls' always fought for toys, and Alex wondered why girls' cannot live in peace.

'Give me my toy,' said Loveth.

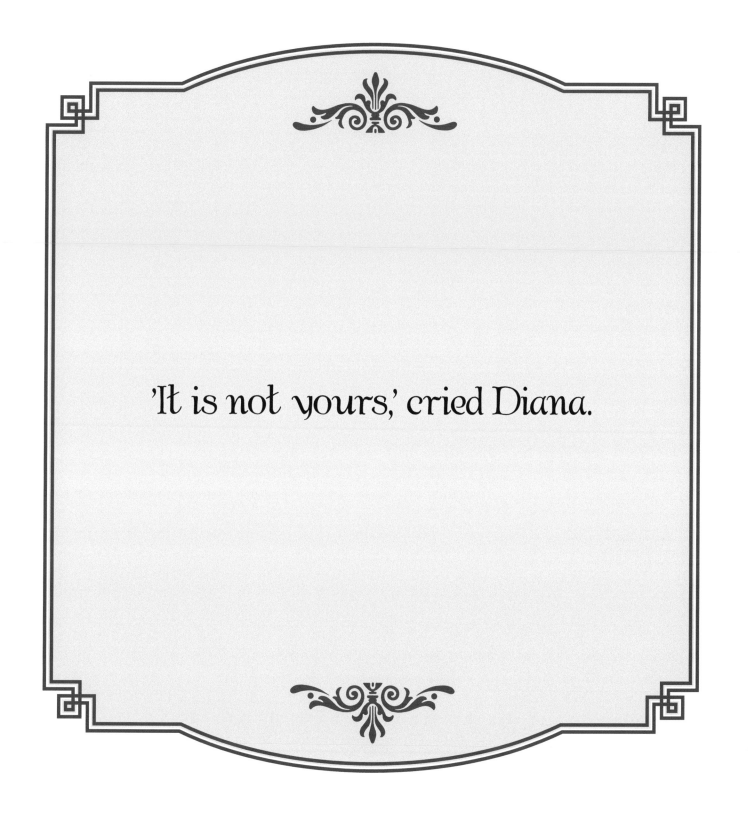

'It is not yours,' cried Diana.

They fell on the floor while dragging for a Cinderella toy who wore a dress with a lovely shoe.

'why do you girls' always fight over toys?' asked Alex.

Diana left the toy for Loveth who was not willing to let go of it.

'I hate you,' cried Loveth.

'You think you are the best and you feel too big because you come first in your class and your homework is great,' said Loveth.

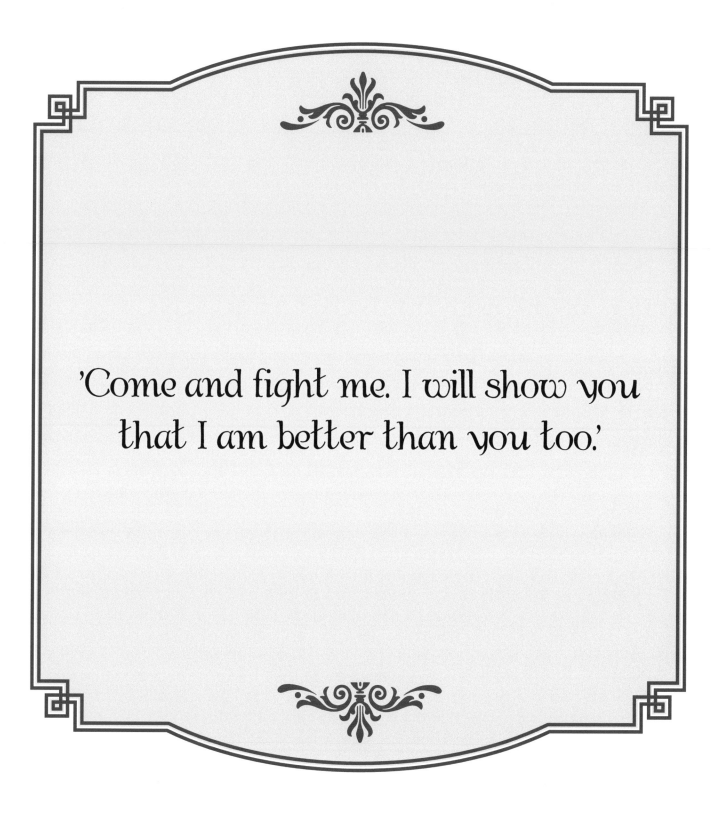

'Come and fight me. I will show you that I am better than you too.'

Alex looked astonished at
the reaction of Loveth, who
was the second child.

He is nine years old. Loveth is seven years old, Diana, their baby sister is five years old.

'I thought you wanted the toy.'
She left it for you to create a
peaceful atmosphere, but you
seem to be angry that she is doing
better in school than yourself.'

'I hate her,' cried Loveth as she threw the toy on the floor.

'I do not hate you,' said little Diana in tears. 'I did not make myself the best in school. I just realised that everything I do turns out great.' She ran to Alex in tears.

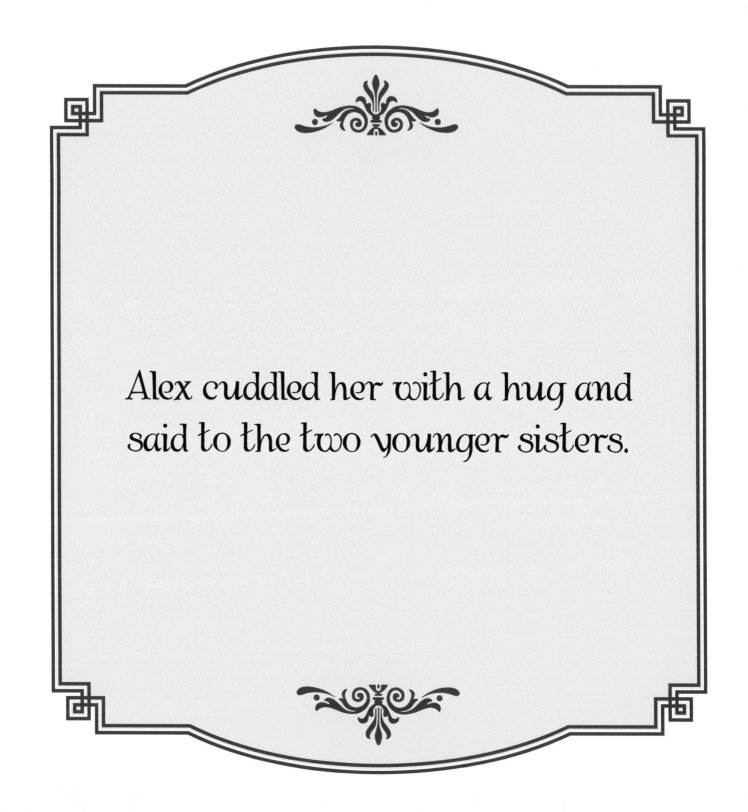

Alex cuddled her with a hug and said to the two younger sisters.

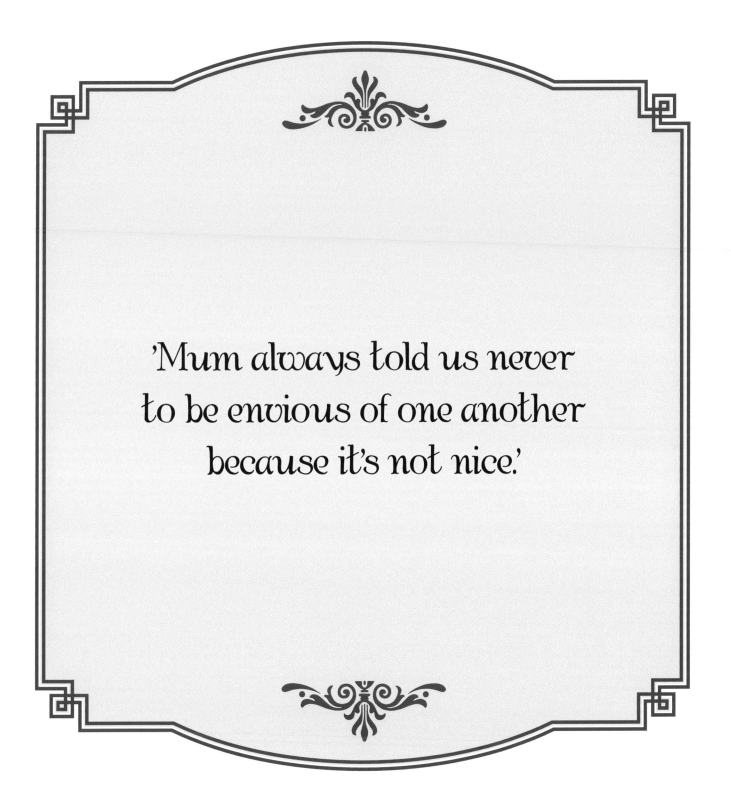

'Mum always told us never to be envious of one another because it's not nice.'

Loveth on hearing these words ran to Diana and said 'I am sorry for mistreating you.' Diana dried her tears and told her that she is happy and that she loves her immensely.

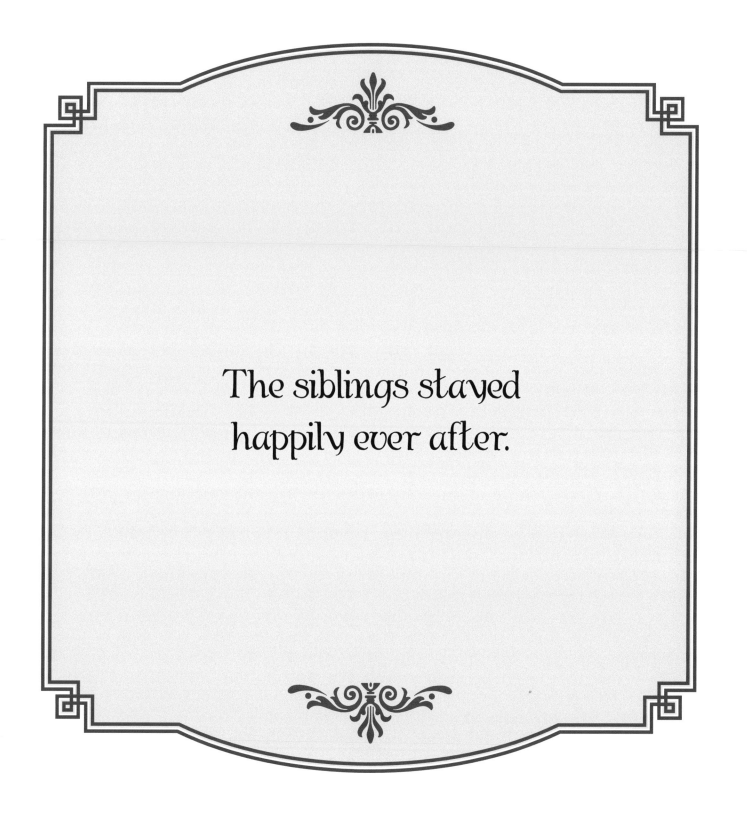

The siblings stayed
happily ever after.

Loving one another is vital to
building a good relationship
in the family and society.

THE END.

Printed in the United States
by Baker & Taylor Publisher Services